Julie Andrews Edwards & Emma Walton Hamilton

Dumpy
the Dump Truck

Illustrated by Tony Walton

Hyperion Books for Children • New York

WAY OUT EAST, WHERE THE COUNTRY MEETS THE SEA, there is a little village called Apple Harbor. Seagulls circling high above the fishing boats can clearly see the stony breakwater and sandy beach, the brightly painted cottages, the church steeple, schoolhouse, and a small whitewashed post office.

Behind the village, overlooking the bay, sits Merryhill Farm.
Most days, Farmer Barnes can be seen driving Trundle the
Tractor up and down the green and golden fields.

"**PUTT-PUTT-PUTT-PUTT!**" Trundle turns over the fresh
earth and plants the potatoes, corn, and wheat. "All in a day's
work," he says.

Nearby, Bee-Bee the Backhoe scoops and dumps, and scoops and dumps . . . digging holes and planting apple trees. "**BEEP! BEEP! BEEP!**" she says as she backs up to scoop once more. "Two hands are better than one!"

"**COCK-A-DOODLE-DOO**!" crowed the rooster on the old barn roof. (He does it every morning.)

As the sun rose over the hill, something twinkled in the tall grass beside the barn. Among the berries and thistles, there was a cracked mirror . . . a flat tire . . . a twisted fender . . . and a sooty smokestack.

What could it possibly be?

It was an old DUMP TRUCK!

The little truck had been there for such a long time that he felt stiff and sore. Birds and mice had used the stuffing from his faded leather seats to build their nests, and he was dusty and very rusty.

BANG! went the back door of the farmhouse. Charlie and his grandfather, Pop-Up, strode across the farmyard.

"But why?" Charlie was saying. "Why do we have to get rid of Dumpy?"

"Because everything's changing around here," said Pop-Up. "The old barn has to come down to make room for a better one, and that little truck is in the way. Besides, you heard your dad—he wants to buy a new one."

"But I love Dumpy," said Charlie. "I play on him every day and pretend that we're driving all over town."

They stood for a moment, gazing at Dumpy.

"It's so sad to get rid of something you love just to make room for something new." Charlie sighed.

"You're right about that," said Pop-Up. "When I ran this farm, Dumpy did everything. And when something broke, you fixed it. You didn't just throw it away."

"Well, why can't we fix Dumpy?" Charlie asked. "And then Dumpy can help Daddy with the new barn!"

Pop-Up pushed back his hat and scratched his head.

"I don't know," he said thoughtfully. "Things are going to be pretty busy around here. And I'm not as quick as I used to be. . . ."

"I can help!" said Charlie. "We could do it in time, I know!"

A slow smile spread across Pop-Up's face. "You know, pal, this might be just the thing I'm looking for. Maybe we could even use Dumpy for odd jobs around town."

So Pop-Up and Charlie went to work.

First they asked Old Nellie, the cart horse, to help pull Dumpy out of the weeds.

Then, Charlie and Pop-Up began to clean. They hosed, scrubbed, wiped, polished, and scraped.

They got rid of all Dumpy's rust and mud, and buffed his old headlights until they gleamed.

There was so much work to do that they had to get up extra early, before farm chores began.

Farmer Barnes often came by on Trundle.

"**PUTT-PUTT-PUTT-PUTT!** All in a day's work!" Trundle would say.

"Looks like you've still got a long way to go," Farmer Barnes fretted. "I hate to remind you, but we don't have much time before that barn has to come down."

"Pshaw!" said Pop-Up. "Just watch our dust!"

The days flew by.

Slowly but surely, Dumpy could feel himself coming back to life. Pop-Up brought Dumpy four fat new tires with shiny hubcaps, and buttery leather seats that smelled like cinnamon toast.

Pop-Up and Charlie spent hours on the dump truck's great bed. The arm that raised it up and down was stuck, and Pop-Up had to use so much grease on it that he was slippery from head to toe.

Next came the part that Dumpy liked best! Pop-Up and Charlie
gave him several coats of paint, in bright and cheerful colors: apple
red, sunshine yellow, ocean blue.

But now Charlie was becoming a little anxious.

"Two more days, Pop-Up, and Dad says the barn *has* to come down!"

Pop-Up's head was buried under Dumpy's hood.

"I've just got to fix the engine!"

CLANG! **BANG!** PING! DING! **POW!** WHEEZE! HISSsssss s s s s s !

Dumpy had a stomachache from all the poking.

"Sorry, Dumpy!" said Pop-Up. "But you can't run without an engine! We've just got to keep at it."

So they worked late into the night.

The next morning, a sleepy Pop-Up said to Charlie, "Okay, pal, let's start him up!" Carefully, he turned the shiny new key in Dumpy's ignition.

"**BANG! PHUT! SPLUTTER!**" coughed Dumpy. He heaved a big sigh.

Silence.

"Now, let's see," said Pop-Up, as he went back under the hood, "a tweak here . . . some oil there." He climbed into the cab and turned the key once again.

"**ERRRRR . . . ERRRRRRR . . . ERRRRRRRRR!**" Dumpy complained.

"Oh, *please*, Dumpy! Please start!" Charlie pleaded.
Dumpy took a deep breath and tried as hard as he could.
POP*!* An old nest exploded out of his smokestack.
Dumpy gave a satisfied burp.
"So *that's* what it was!" Pop-Up smiled. "Dumpy must be feeling much better now!"

He turned the key one last time. Dumpy was feeling just grand, and he roared with happiness.

"**BRRROOOOM! BRRROOOOOMMM!**"

"YES!" Charlie yelled.

"YES!" yelled Pop-Up.

"What is it? What's happened?" Farmer Barnes barreled around the corner on Trundle, and slammed on the brakes. Trundle stalled, and for once was speechless.

There was Dumpy—mint-fresh and sparkling, his engine humming happily.

"Well, what are we waiting for?" Pop-Up winked at Farmer Barnes. "Let's get to work on that barn!"

So, with Dumpy's help, the old barn came tumbling down.

Dumpy hauled timbers and helped stack them for later use. He fetched bricks and wood, and delivered huge bags of cement and gravel. Every day, he grew stronger and stronger.

Word of Dumpy's return spread,

and all sorts of people came to see him at work.

Stinky the Garbage Truck drove into the yard, and was amazed to see Dumpy lifting and tipping load after load.

"**ERR-RNN**!" he said happily. "It's not what you do, it's *how* you do it!"

Bee-Bee the Backhoe dug a big hole for the new barn's foundation.

"**BEEP! BEEP! BEEP!**" she said as she scooped and dumped the earth into Dumpy, who carted it all away. "Two hands are better than one!"

Pop-Up tied a strong rope to Dumpy's fender, and with Trundle's help they raised the sides of the new barn. "All in a day's work," said Trundle proudly.

The day came when the last shingle was nailed to the
roof. Farmer Barnes stepped back to admire the new barn.

"Well, I take it all back." He put his arm around Charlie's shoulders,
and smiled at Pop-Up. "You guys make a great team. Tomorrow, we'll

start the harvest . . . and after that, who knows? Dumpy could be the busiest truck in town!"

"**DING-A-LING-A-LING**!" Ike the Ice Cream Truck drove into the farmyard. "You're in for a treat!" he called.

"Ice cream for everyone!" declared Farmer Barnes.

That night, Pop-Up and Charlie put Dumpy to bed inside the cozy new barn. It smelled of hay and herbs, fresh wood, and a hint of Dumpy's gasoline.

"Time for us to get to bed, too," said Pop-Up.

"Good job, Dumpy . . ." Charlie whispered, rubbing a fender gently with his sleeve. "We couldn't have done it without you."

The barn doors swung closed.

Dumpy heaved a happy, sleepy sigh. He knew *he* couldn't have done any of it without Charlie and Pop-Up.

For Sam, of course.

All rights reserved.
No part of this book may be reproduced or transmitted
in any form or by any means, electronic or mechanical, including
photocopying, recording, or by any information storage and
retrieval system, without written permission from the publisher.
For information address Hyperion Books for Children,
114 Fifth Avenue, New York, New York 10011-5690.

Printed in the USA

This book is set in 18-point Cochin.
The artwork for each picture was prepared using watercolor and colored pencil.

FIRST EDITION

3 5 7 9 10 8 6 4 2

Library of Congress Cataloging-in-Publication Data on file.

Visit www.hyperionchildrensbooks.com